Stuart Trotter

My Perfect
Pet

My perfect pet...

is dry, not wet,

is not

too small...

...and not too **tall**

He's not too hairy...

and not too scary!

He's not
too grimey...

and not too slimey!

Not too leathery,

...and not too feathery.

He's not too jumpy...

and not too bumpy.

He's
not
too
slinky...

and not too stinky!

He's not too cheeky...

and not
too squeaky.

He's not too spiny...

and not at all shiny!

He's not too snappy...

but is very happy!

Can you guess what I've got?

I'm sure you'll never have met...

such a wonderfully...

...perfect pet!

First published in 2015 by © Rockpool Children's Books Ltd.

This edition published in 2017 by Rockpool Children's Books
Ltd. in association with Albury Books.
Albury Court, Albury, Thame
OX9 2LP, United Kingdom

Text copyright © Stuart Trotter 2015
Illustrations copyright © Stuart Trotter 2015

The rights of Stuart Trotter to be identified as
the author and illustrator have been asserted by him
in accordance with the Copyright, Designs and Patents Act, 1988

A CIP catalogue record of this book is available
from the British Library.
All rights reserved

Printed in China
ISBN 978-1-906081-92-8

rockpool
children's books

Albury Books